Christmas at the Top of the World

WRITTEN & ILLUSTRATED BY

Tim Coffey

ALBERT WHITMAN & COMPANY, MORTON GROVE, ILLINOIS

Library of Congress Cataloging-in-Publication Data

Coffey, Tim.
Christmas at the top of the world / written and illustrated by Tim Coffey.
p. cm.
Summary: On Christmas Eve, a young reindeer travels through the woods
leading a procession of animals to the top of the earth, where a special old man awaits.
ISBN 0-8075-5762-5 (hardcover)
[1. Reindeer—Fiction. 2. Animals—Fiction. 3. Santa Claus—Fiction. 4.Christmas—Fiction] I. Title.
PZ7.C6585Ch 2003 [E]—dc21 2003001151

The paintings were rendered in acrylic on watercolor paper textured with gesso.
The design is by Carol Gildar.

For more information about Albert Whitman & Company,
visit our web site at www.albertwhitman.com.

In memory of Dan

Littile Reindeer loved winter. That was because Papa would tell him his favorite story at sleep time.

"When I was your age, I discovered a place where the ground rises up to the sky and you are high enough to touch the stars," Papa said. "A magical place, at the top of the world."

Where could this be?
Little Reindeer wondered.
He would wonder every night until he fell asleep.

One frosty night, Papa told Mama and Little Reindeer he was going on a journey.

"I'm leaving tomorrow," he said gently, "but I'll be back on Christmas."

Little Reindeer's ears perked up. "I want to go, too!" he said.

"One day you'll go," said Papa. "Just wait."

In the morning, Little Reindeer and Mama kissed Papa goodbye and watched him disappear deep into the woods. Little Reindeer had lots of questions.

"Where did Papa go?" he asked Mama. "How long until he's back? How long until Christmas?"

"He's up north, at the top of the world," Mama replied. "And when the north wind feels warm and smells sweet, it'll be Christmas Eve. You'll know," she added. "All the animals will know."

It was hard to wait for Papa. At night, while Mama slept, Little Reindeer stared at the sky. He remembered Papa's story about a magical place. *A place where you are high enough to touch the stars.* Days and days passed, and then—one night felt different.

The air smelled warm and sweet. It was the wind from the north. "The top of the world," he whispered. That was where Papa was, right now.

It was Christmas Eve. Little Reindeer couldn't wait anymore. He was going to find Papa!

The other animals saw him go.

Little Reindeer walked for a long time.
At last he turned to look back. Every creature of the North
Woods was behind him. And Mama, too!

He remembered what she'd said about Christmas Eve:
All the animals will know. Now they were following Little Reindeer
to the top of the world.

At the top of a hill, Little Reindeer stopped, and the other animals stopped, too.

They heard only silence, and then they saw the place
where the earth touched the heavens.

There were green stars, red stars, blue stars, too—yellow and white twinkling stars—they were close enough to touch, just as Papa had said.

Little Reindeer made his way toward the biggest, brightest star.

In the center of the village, the star glittered and shone at the top of a beautiful tree. It was like no other star Little Reindeer had ever seen.

"But where is Papa?" he wondered.

He could hear bells jingling up in the sky. Something was coming—he could hear it louder and closer. Something big! In a flash, it swooped down to the ground.

What was it? The other animals gathered around, and Little Reindeer nudged his way to the front of the crowd.

An old man came
over to Little Reindeer,
knelt down, and patted
his head softly.

"I know who you are,"
the man said with a twinkle
in his eye. "You must be
here to see your papa."

Ａnd that's when Little Reindeer saw Papa by the sleigh. Papa was leading all the other reindeer!

"This is the magic place, isn't it?" whispered Little Reindeer. "I couldn't wait."

"You waited as long as you could," said Papa. "It's Christmas Eve."

It was time for the kind old man, Papa, and the other reindeer to bring the peace and magic of this place to the rest of the world.

Little Reindeer stood with Mama and watched Papa soar above the village into the snowy night.

Then he snuggled against Mama and fell asleep.
It would be Christmas soon, and Little Reindeer was
on top of the world.